WITHDRAWN

DREW BARRYMORE

A Real-Life Reader Biography

Susan Zannos

Mitchell Lane Publishers, Inc.
P.O. Box 619 • Bear, Delaware 19701

First Printing

Real-Life Reader Biographies

Selena
Tommy Nuñez
Oscar De La Hoya
Cesar Chavez
Vanessa Williams
Brandy
Garth Brooks
Sheila E.
Arnold Schwarzenegger
Steve Jobs
Jennifer Love Hewitt
Melissa Joan Hart
Winona Ryder
Christina Aguilera
Robert Rodriguez
Trent Dimas
Gloria Estefan
Chuck Norris
Celine Dion
Michelle Kwan
Jeff Gordon
Hollywood Hogan
Jennifer Lopez
Sandra Bullock
Keri Russell
Drew Barrymore
Alyssa Milano
Mariah Carey
Cristina Saralegui
Jimmy Smits
Sinbad
Mia Hamm
Rosie O'Donnell
Mark McGwire
Ricky Martin
Kobe Bryant
Julia Roberts
Sarah Michelle Gellar
Alicia Silverstone
Freddie Prinze, Jr.
Rafael Palmeiro
Andres Galarraga
Mary Joe Fernandez
Paula Abdul
Sammy Sosa
Shania Twain
Salma Hayek
Britney Spears
Derek Jeter
Robin Williams
Liv Tyler
Katie Holmes
Enrique Iglesias

Library of Congress Cataloging-in-Publication Data
Zannos, Susan.
Drew Barrymore/Susan Zannos.
p. cm.—(A real-life reader biography)
Includes index.
Filmography:
ISBN 1-58415-035-1
1. Barrymore, Drew—Juvenile literature. 2. Motion picture actors and actresses—United States—Biography—Juvenile literature. [1. Barrymore, Drew. 2. Actors and actresses. 3. Women—Biography.] I. Title. II. Series.
PN2287.B29 Z36 2000
791.43'028'092—dc21
[B]

00-036532

ABOUT THE AUTHOR: Susan Zannos has taught at all levels, from preschool to college, in Mexico, Greece, Italy, Russia, and Lithuania, as well as in the United States. She has published a mystery *Trust the Liar* (Walker and Co.) and *Human Types: Essence and the Enneagram* was published by Samuel Weiser in 1997. She has written several books for children, including *Paula Abdul* and *Cesar Chavez* (Mitchell Lane).

PHOTO CREDITS: cover: Kobal Collection; p. 4 Victor Malafronte/Archive Photos; p. 6 Globe Photos; p. 7 Bettman/Corbis; p. 9 Universal/Fotos International/Archive Photos; p. 10 Fotos International/Archive Photos; p. 19 Richard Corkery/Corbis; p. 24 Marty Lederhandler/AP Photo; p. 25, 28 Kobal Collection

ACKNOWLEDGMENTS: The following story has been thoroughly researched, and to the best of our knowledge, represents a true story. While every possible effort has been made to ensure accuracy, the publisher will not assume liability for damages caused by inaccuracies in the data, and makes no warranty on the accuracy of the information contained herein. This story has not been authorized nor endorsed by Drew Barrymore.

Table of Contents

Chapter 1
A Star is Born

Drew Barrymore was born into a family of famous actors. Like other famous Barrymores, Drew is talented and intelligent. Also like other Barrymores, she has had serious problems with alcohol and drugs.

Like other famous Barry–mores, Drew is talented and intelligent.

Drew was born on February 22, 1975. Her mother, Jaid, and her father, John Drew Barrymore, were already separated. Jaid had come to Hollywood with dreams of becoming a movie star. She had a job as a waitress when the handsome actor John Barrymore came into the nightclub where she worked.

Drew with her mother Jaid and father John in front of Barrymore Theatre in New York.

When Jaid married him, he was already an alcoholic who had been arrested many times for the use of drugs and alcohol. Jaid and John Barrymore had violent fights. Because Jaid realized this was not a good environment for a child, she knew she had to leave her husband and raise her child alone.

It was very hard for Jaid Barrymore to earn a living. She still had her dreams of being in movies, but it was her job as a waitress that paid the rent. Jaid tried out for acting jobs during the day and worked at night. Baby Drew spent all her time with babysitters.

Jaid's friends told her that baby Drew was so beautiful she should be in commercials. One friend took a picture of the baby and sent it to an agent. The agent called, but Jaid said she didn't want her daughter in show business. The agent wouldn't give up. Finally Jaid agreed to take 11-month-old Drew for an interview. When Jaid and Drew got to the big Hollywood soundstage, it was full of hundreds of babies being tested for a puppy food commercial. Each baby took a turn playing with a puppy. Some babies cried. Some babies just sat and did nothing. Drew laughed and played with the puppy. She got the job!

When Drew was two and a half years old, she was in a made-for-TV movie called *Suddenly Love.* By the time she was four years old, she told her mother, "I really want to act. I like it so much."

Jaid was astonished at her daughter's success.

At the age of four, Drew hugs her mother Jaid.

She had tried out for dozens of roles without being chosen. Drew was hired for the first four commercials and the first feature film she auditioned for. This feature film, *Altered States,* was made in 1980, when Drew was five years old.

When Drew was seven years old, she became a star.

When she was home, Drew was very lonely. She longed to be part of a family. But she hardly knew her father, and she was afraid of him because she had seen his drunken episodes of violent anger. Her mother was still gone all day and most of the night, working.

When Drew was seven years old, she became a star. She played the part of Gertie in one of the most popular films ever made, *E.T.: The Extra-Terrestrial.* The cast and film crew of *E.T.* became Drew's family. Director Steven Spielberg was like a father to her. She would go to his house on weekends. The boys who played her brothers in the movie were like real brothers. And Drew loved E.T. She would take her lunch into the room where the alien model was kept and talk to it. When the film was released, Drew

Her role in the movie E.T. *made Drew famous.*

became famous. She traveled all over making publicity appearances with the other cast members.

Drew continued to work steadily in the 1980s. Only when she was working on a movie did she feel like she really belonged. The problem was that when the filming was done, Drew's "family" ended, too. She starred in feature films like *Firestarter,* in which she had the leading role as a little girl who could

Drew was well-known everywhere she went.

start fires with her mind. In *Irreconcilable Differences* she played the part of a child who "divorced" her parents for neglect. She was nominated for a Golden Globe award for this role.

Drew was making enough money that Jaid Barrymore was able to quit her other jobs and be Drew's manager. That turned out to be a big mistake. Drew needed a mother more than she needed a manager.

Chapter 2
Party Girl

Drew liked acting because when she was working on a movie set, she felt like she belonged. She liked being a star for the same reason. When she and her mother would go to Hollywood parties, publicity events, and clubs, she would be accepted because she was Drew Barrymore, the celebrity. Even though she was often the youngest person at parties, everyone knew her. She belonged.

Even though she was often the youngest person at parties, everyone knew her.

Drew and her best friend, the daughter of one of Jaid's friends, started smoking when Drew was nine years old. The two little girls would go to their favorite club with their mothers. Then they would run off together and smoke in the rest room. Before long they started drinking, too. They would watch until someone left a drink sitting on a table. Then they would run and grab the glass and finish the drink. Sometimes they would ask one of the young men to let them have a drink of his beer. The men thought it was cute.

Drew began to think that she couldn't have fun without drinking.

Even after Drew had had so much to drink that she could hardly walk, her mother didn't realize what was going on. She thought her daughter was just tired from being out so late. One time when Jaid thought Drew smelled like beer, Drew told her mother that a boy had given her one sip. Drew was such a good actress that she fooled her mother.

Before long, Drew began to think that she couldn't have fun without drinking. At the same time, she was getting fewer parts. She was at an age where she was too old to play a cute little kid and too young to play a teen.

Without her acting to keep her busy, she became more and more desperate to go out at night and party.

Drew had a few close friends who all hated school. They liked to sleep over at each other's houses on weekends so that they could smoke and sneak liquor from their parents' cupboards. They liked to stay out late at the fashionable clubs. The mother of one of these girls offered Drew her first marijuana cigarette one night when Drew was staying at their house. Drew soon found that she liked to smoke pot, too.

When Drew was 11 years old, Jaid enrolled her in a different private school. At first Drew didn't want to go to a new school, but she soon changed her mind. It wasn't because she liked the new teachers. What she liked was being in a school that had classes all the way through high school. Even though Drew was only in sixth grade, she made friends who were high-school seniors.

Even though Drew was only in sixth grade, she made friends who were high-school seniors.

Drew's new friends smoked pot and drank, like she did. They had their

Drew was so dependent on alcohol and marijuana that she wasn't even interested in acting.

own cars and could drive wherever they wanted to. She skipped school with them to smoke and drink. Even though Drew was much younger, she was accepted as part of the gang because she was a celebrity and had a lot of experience. The more time Drew spent with her new friends, the more she hated her mother's rules. Soon Drew and her mother were fighting all the time.

When Drew was cast in *See You in the Morning,* a movie that was going to be made in New York, she didn't want to go. She was so dependent on alcohol and marijuana that she wasn't even interested in acting. She was afraid she wouldn't be able to drink and smoke if she left her gang of friends. But her agent and her mother, who was also her manager, insisted that she go. Acting had been the most important thing in Drew's life. Now it didn't seem important to her.

Drew felt that her mother was her enemy. She thought that her mother only wanted the money she could earn. All Drew wanted was freedom—freedom to stay out as late as she wanted and to drink and smoke whenever she felt like it. And she felt like it all the time.

It didn't take her very long to find new friends in New York who would party with her. Many of Drew's New York friends used cocaine. When Drew got back to Los Angeles, she started using cocaine, too.

It didn't take Drew very long to find new friends in New York who would party with her.

Chapter 3
Recovery

Drew's mother finally realized that something was very wrong. One of Drew's friends had gone to a treatment center for alcohol and drug abuse. Of course Drew didn't see that girl anymore. But Jaid talked to the girl's mother. One night when Drew came home very drunk, Jaid and the girl's mother took Drew to the treatment center.

Drew was very frightened, but she knew she needed help.

Drew was very frightened, but she knew she needed help. At only 13 years old, she was addicted to alcohol and drugs. She felt that no one could understand her. At the ASAP Family Treatment Center, she met other teenagers who were also alcoholics and drug users. She found out that she wasn't that different just because she was a movie star. Other young people had problems with their families and with drinking and doing drugs.

Drew also found out more about her own famous family, the Barrymores. Of course she had heard about them from other people in show business, but her mother never wanted to talk about them. Drew learned that not only were the Barrymores famous American actors, many were also alcoholics. Her grandfather, John Barrymore, had been a star in movies and the theater. His sister Ethel Barrymore and his brother Lionel Barrymore were also famous actors. Drew's grandfather died of alcoholism with only 60 cents in his pocket. His daughter, Drew's aunt, was Diana Barrymore. She wrote about her problems with alcohol and drugs in her book *Too Much, Too Soon*. Diana died

Drew's grandfather died of alcoholism with only 60 cents in his pocket.

when she was only 38. Diana's younger brother, John Barrymore, Jr., was Drew's father, an alcoholic who could no longer work because of his addiction.

Just as Drew was beginning to learn about herself and her family, she had to leave the treatment center.

Just as Drew was beginning to learn about herself and her family, she had to leave the treatment center. She had a contract to make a movie, *Far from Home,* in Nevada. Drew's mother promised she would return to the treatment center as soon as the movie was finished. Drew did go back, but soon she had to leave again to go to New York.

In New York, Drew began seeing her old friends. She started using cocaine again. Drew and a friend stole one of her mother's credit cards and got on an airplane for Los Angeles. The two girls planned to go to Hawaii. Drew's mother called some agents in Los Angeles who found Drew and took her back to the ASAP treatment center in handcuffs. This time the people at the center insisted that Drew had to stay. There would be no more leaving to make movies. Drew's recovery had become the most important thing in her life.

Drew made a lot of progress. She had group therapy, private treatment, family therapy with her mother, and counseling sessions. Then, just before she was to be released in December, *The National Enquirer,* a tabloid newspaper, found out that she was in treatment. Drew decided to tell her own story in *People* magazine. She also wrote a book about her life, *Little Girl Lost.* The writer from the magazine, Todd Gold, helped her write the book. It became a best-seller.

Although their relationship changed through the years, Drew remained close with her mother.

But Drew's problems weren't over. When she was 14 years old, she attempted suicide by cutting her wrists. She was rushed to a hospital emergency room. After that she spent more time in the treatment center. For nearly a year after her release, she lived with rock star David Crosby and his wife, Jan. Drew said later, "They made me believe that there actually were trustworthy people out there."

When Drew was 14 years old, she attempted suicide by cutting her wrists.

When Drew was 15 years old, she went through the legal process to declare herself independent of her parents. For a long time she did not have any contact with her mother. It was hard for Drew to earn money because she was not offered any parts in movies. She worked as a waitress in a coffee shop. People in Hollywood thought her acting career was over. They were wrong.

Chapter 4
Comeback

For nearly two years—1990 and most of 1991—Drew could not find any work. But she didn't give up. She kept trying out for parts. She said later, "People wouldn't touch me; they just thought I was some loser drug addict."

Finally, Drew got the break she needed. People around Hollywood had noticed that she was clean and sober. When she tried out for the lead part in the movie *Poison Ivy,* she was sure she would get it. She did. The story was about a treacherous teenage murderess.

Finally, Drew got the break she needed.

Other parts soon followed. In one year, 1992, Drew made five feature films

The newspapers and magazines called Drew "wild child."

and a made-for-TV movie. She also appeared in a television series called *2000 Malibu Road.*

Her movies got good reviews. In the movie *Guncrazy* (1992), she played the part of a wayward teenager in love with an ex-convict. A critic in *The New York Times* wrote that she was "enchanting to watch, both angelic and monstrous." She was nominated again for a Golden Globe award for this role. She played another murderous teenager in the TV movie *The Amy Fisher Story* (1993), which was based on the true story of a girl who attempted to murder her lover's wife. In the movie *Bad Girls* (1994), Drew played a teenage prostitute in the old West who was out for revenge.

Drew was playing the roles of bad girls in her movies. She was playing the role of a bad girl in her life, too. The newspapers and magazines called her "wild child." But there was a difference now. She wasn't using alcohol and drugs. She was doing things that shocked people, but not things that hurt herself or anyone else.

She got some tattoos, a butterfly on her stomach and a cross on her leg. Sometimes she took her clothes off in public. On a late-night TV talk show she lifted her shirt and showed her breasts. She was photographed for a feature in *Playboy* magazine without any clothes on at all.

In an interview for *Rolling Stone* magazine, Drew explained, "I'm an adult, and I'm a child. . . . I get to be a kid now because I wasn't a kid when I was supposed to be one. But in some ways, I'm an old woman—lived it, seen it, done it, been there, have the T-shirt."

Even though Drew made headlines for doing crazy stunts, she always put her acting career first. She said, "Ask any person in this industry if I was ever unprofessional or threw a temper tantrum or walked onto the set drunk. It's never happened. Doesn't that stand for something?"

Even though Drew made headlines for doing crazy stunts, she always put her acting career first.

In addition to her successful comeback in films, Drew also became a model. She was selected as the new GUESS Girl in 1993, wearing the famous jeans and very little else. She was 5′4″ tall and weighed 98 pounds. With her slight figure and sexy good looks, she soon became a favorite with fashion photographers.

Drew finally regained her popularity as an actress.

She was also a favorite with Jeremy Thomas, a Los Angeles bar owner from Wales. Drew had been dating Jeremy for only six weeks when she decided to marry him. It was after midnight on March 20, 1994. Some of their friends called a 24-hour wedding hot line. The minister, who was also a psychic, came to the bar and married Drew and Jeremy at 5:00 A.M. A few hours later Drew had to leave for Tucson, Arizona, where she was making the movie *Boys on the Side.*

Drew worked with Whoopi Goldberg and Matthew McConaughey in Boys on the Side.

Drew later said she had only married Jeremy Thomas so that he would be able to stay in the United States. They were married for six weeks and together for only two days. The brief marriage seemed to cause Drew to be more thoughtful about her actions. She admitted that it had been a mistake. By the time she was 20 years old, she was starting to behave more like an adult than like an irresponsible child.

Chapter 5
Grown Up

Drew wanted to control her own career.

When Drew Barrymore was a lonely child, and when she was a troubled teenager, what she wanted most was to be grown up. She wanted to be free to make her own decisions. She wanted to control her own career. She thought that if she were grown up, everything would be better. It looks like she was right.

Acting continues to be Drew's passion. Since turning 20 in 1995, she has made multiple feature films every year. Although some of her movies have not been successful, Drew has been.

Even when the critics didn't like a movie, they liked Drew's acting.

As an adult actress, Drew has had many different parts. She is no longer cast in only bad-girl roles. In Woody Allen's musical comedy *Everyone Says I Love You* (1996), Drew actually had a singing part. In *Never Been Kissed* (1999) Drew played the part of a mousey newspaper editor who returned to high school to do an undercover story. The beautiful Drew Barrymore managed to look like a clumsy nerd! In *The Wedding Singer,* Drew was as wholesome as a daisy (her favorite flower) in the part of a bride-to-be who nearly marries the wrong man.

Even when the critics didn't like a movie, they liked Drew's acting.

Nowadays it is not Drew who is trying to get the part in the movie, but movie companies that are trying to get Drew. Hollywood producers and directors know that the screen lights up with a special magic when Drew Barrymore is on it. *Ever After,* a lovely 1998 retelling of the Cinderella story, received rave reviews from critics and

Drew produced and starred in the movie Never Been Kissed.

was a box-office hit. It was Drew's version of Cinderella as a charming and honest country girl that made the movie successful.

Drew founded her own production company, Flower Films, in 1994. She was the executive producer of *Like a*

Lady (1996) and *Never Been Kissed*. In a recent interview, Drew said, "I like making movies, so I want to make good movies. I want to swim in a creative pool with wonderful people. And as a producer, I want to create a great working atmosphere for people, and I know how to do that. It's in my blood and in my bones." The year 2000 saw Drew appearing in several more films.

Instead of doing wild things that call attention to herself, Drew has been helping others.

The great acting tradition of the famous Barrymores is carried on by Drew Barrymore. But she is breaking the tradition of addiction and out-of-control behavior that has destroyed many of her relatives. She said, "Unfortunately, I'm not going to take my clothes off anymore. I don't do wild things anymore."

Instead of doing wild things that call attention to herself, Drew has been helping others. She understands now that alcoholism is a disease, not something her family should be blamed for. She has been helping to support her father, John Barrymore. Drew also

Drew Barrymore no longer feels insecure.

donates time and money to charities. She is the spokesperson for the nonprofit Female Health Foundation. She works on the foundation's campaign to promote safe sex. Drew's love of animals finds expression in her support of The Wildlife Waystation. Her concern for children is obvious from her support of the Pediatric AIDS Foundation.

In July 2000, publicist Eddie Michaels announced that Drew and shock-comic Tom Green were engaged. Drew Barrymore no longer feels insecure. She says, "I've been through way too much . . . to be insecure. I've been humbled. That makes you grateful for every day you have."

Filmography

1978	*Suddenly Love* (TV)
1980	*Bogie* (TV)
	Altered States
1982	*E.T.: The Extra-Terrestrial*
1984	*Firestarter*
	Irreconcilable Differences
1985	*Cat's Eye*
1986	*Babes in Toyland*
1987	*Conspiracy of Love* (TV)
1989	*See You in the Morning*
	Far from Home
1991	*Motorama*
1992	*Poison Ivy*
	Waxwork II: Lost in Time
	No Place to Hide
	Guncrazy
	Sketch Artist
	2000 Malibu Road (TV Series)
1993	*Doppelganger: The Evil Within*
	The Amy Fisher Story (TV)
	Wayne's World 2
1994	*Inside the Goldmine*
	Bad Girls
1995	*Boys on the Side*
	Mad Love
	Batman Forever
1996	*Like a Lady*
	Everyone Says I Love You
	Scream
1997	*Wishful Thinking*
	All She Wanted
	Best Men
1998	*Home Fries*
	Ever After
	The Wedding Singer
1999	*Never Been Kissed*
2000	*Charlie's Angels: The Movie*
	Titan A.E. (Voice)
	Skipped Parts

Chronology

1975 Drew Blyth Barrymore born on February 22 in Culver City, California, to Jaid and John Barrymore
1976 Cast in puppy food commercial (January)
1978 Cast in her first made-for-television movie, *Suddenly Love*
1980 Appears in her first feature film, *Altered States*
1982 Becomes a child star when *E.T.: The Extra-Terrestrial* is released
1985 Nominated for a Golden Globe award for best supporting actress in *Irreconcilable Differences*
1988 Admitted to the ASAP Family Treatment Center in Van Nuys for alcohol and drug abuse
1990 Goes through legal process to declare emancipation from her parents; writes autobiography, *Little Girl Lost,* with Todd Gold
1994 Marries Welsh bar owner Jeremy Thomas on March 20; they are divorced after six weeks of marriage; forms her own production company, Flower Films
1995 Appears nude in *Playboy* magazine
1999 Wins Actress of the Year at the Hollywood Film Festival; her baby clothes are auctioned off by her mother

Index